NICARAGUA

MAJOR WORLD NATIONS
NICARAGUA

John Griffiths

CHELSEA HOUSE PUBLISHERS
Philadelphia

Chelsea House Publishers

First Printing.

1 3 5 7 9 8 6 4 2

Library of Congress Cataloging-in-Publication Data

Griffiths, John. 1942 Apr. 5-
Nicaragua / John Griffiths.
p. cm. — (Major world nations)
Includes index.
Summary: Describes the history, geography, climate, economy,
religion, culture and people of Nicaragua.
ISBN 0-7910-4976-0
1. Nicaragua—Juvenile literature. [1. Nicaragua.] I. Title.
II. Series.
F1523.2.675 1998
972.85—dc21   98-6399
CIP
AC

ACKNOWLEDGEMENTS

The Author and Publishers are grateful to the following individuals and organizations
for permission to reproduce the illustrations in this book:
Camerapix Hutchison, Mike Goldwater/Oxfam, The Mansell Collection Limited,
Paul Morris, Nicaragua Solidarity Campaign, Anthony Pike, Carlos Reyes/Andes
Press Agency, Tove Tomic/Andes Press Agency, Travel Photo International,
Photothéque Vautier-de Nanxe, and Associated Press.
Extracts from the *New York Times*. Copyright © 1972/79 by The New York Times
Company, reprinted by permission.
Poems reprinted by permission of MEP Publications.

CONTENTS

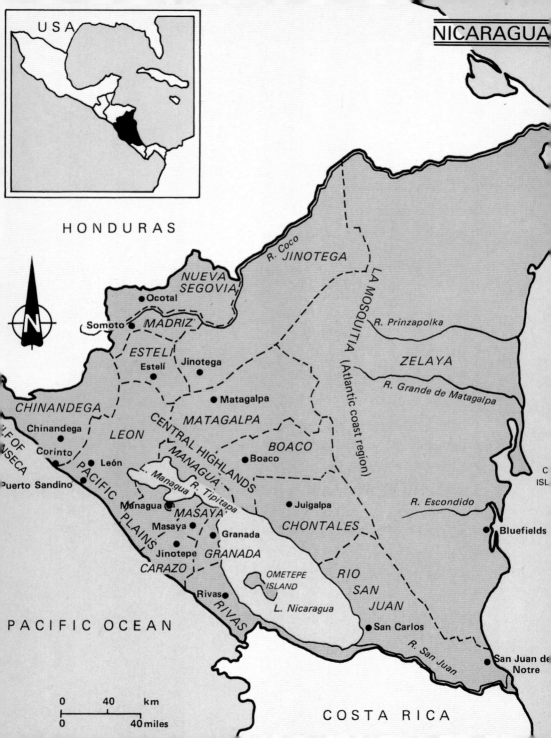

FACTS AT A GLANCE

Land and People

Official Name	Republic of Nicaragua (República de Nicaragua)
Location	Central America, south of Honduras, north of Costa Rica
Area	50,464 square miles (130,700 square kilometers)
Climate	Tropical
Capital	Managua
Other Cities	León, Chinandega, Masaya, Granada, Esteli
Population	4,632,000
Population Density	98.8 persons per square mile (38.1 persons per square kilometer)
Major Rivers	Coco, San Juan
Major Lakes	Lake Nicaragua, Lake Managua
Mountains	Volcan Momotombo, Volcan Concepcion, Volcan Madera, Volcan Mombacho
Official Language	Spanish

Religions	Roman Catholic, Protestant
Literacy Rate	65.7 percent
Average Life Expectancy	63.4 years for males; 68.1 years for females

Economy

Natural Resources	Farmland, gold , silver
Division of Labor Force	Agriculture (80 percent); light industry (10 percent
Agricultural Products	Coffee, sugar, maize(corn), cotton
Other Products	Shellfish, beef, gold, silver
Industries	Agriculture, mining, light industry (processing raw materials)
Major Imports	Manufactured goods, petroleum
Major Exports	Coffee, shellfish, beef, sugar
Currency	Cordobo oro

Government

Form of Government	Constitutional republic
Government Bodies	National Assembly
Formal Head of State	President

HISTORY AT A GLANCE

1000 A.D. Nahuatl-speakers, related to the Aztecs of Mexico, arrive in the region.

1502 Christopher Columbus sails along Nicaragua's Caribbean coast during his fourth voyage.

1524 An expedition is sent to colonize the region, under Francisco Hernandez de Cordoba. The towns of León and Grenada are founded.

1610 León is buried by a volcanic eruption.

1780 A British expedition under the young Horatio Nelson attempts to row up the San Juan River to attack Spanish settlements on Lake Nicaragua. The expedition is eventually defeated by disease, bad weather and difficult terrain.

1783 As a result of the Treaty of Paris between Great Britain and the newly-independent United States, English settlements on the Caribbean coast of Central America survive. Nicaragua does not achieve full sovereignty over its English-speaking Mosquito Coast until 1894.

1812 The country's first university is founded in León.

1821   Nicaragua, along with most of Latin America, achieves independence from Spain.

1823   United Provinces of Central America formed on July 1, including Guatemala, El Salvador, Honduras, Nicaragua, and Costa Rica.

1838   After years of dissension, the United Provinces breaks up into separate nations.

1857   Managua selected as national capital as compromise between León, the former capital, and Grenada.

1907   During the brief Nicaragua–Honduras war Nicaraguan forces occupy the Honduran capital.

1912   The United States dispatches a Marine force to Nicaragua during a period of unrest. U.S. forces remain in the country for 20 years.

1933   U.S. forces withdraw, but leave behind a new National Guard which they have organized, under the command of Anastasio Somoza Garcia.

1934   Opposition leader Augusto C. Sandino is assassinated by Somoza forces.

1937   Anastasio Somoza elected president. He rules Nicaragua for 20 years, amassing a large personal fortune.

1956   Anastasio Somoza is assassinated, but soon replaced by his son Luis Somoza Debayle.

1961   Nicaraguan exiles found the FSLN (Frente Sandinista de Liberacion National, or Sandinista National Liberation Front). They take their name from Augusto C. Sandino, the opposition leader assassinated in 1934.

1963	The FSLN begins guerrilla operations in rural areas.
1965	The poet and priest Ernesto Cardenal establishes his religious community at Solentiname in Lake Nicaragua.
1967	A broad-based uprising against the Somoza regime fails. Luis Somoza dies and is replaced by his brother Anastasio Somoza Debayle.
1972	A large earthquake strikes Nicaragua damaging many historic buildings in Managua.
1976-1978	The struggle against the Somoza regime grows and opposition leaders are killed.
1979	Somoza is driven from power and replaced by an interim government dominated by the Sandinistas. Non-Sandinista members of the government soon resign. Relations with the U.S. decline after the Sandinistas are accused of supplying rebels in El Salvador.
1980s	The United States supports the "Contra" war fought against the Sandinistas from bases in Honduras and Costa Rica. Thousands of U.S.-backed rebels and Sandinista supporters are eventually killed.
1984	An election is held but most non-Sandinista groups refuse to participate.
1990	A large anti-Sandinista coalition forms as another election approaches. Violetta de Barrios Chomorro and the UNO coalition win the presidency and a majority in the legislature.
1991-1995	Settlements are negotiated in most of the ongoing civil wars in Central America.

1996 New elections are held. The coaliton, now led by Arnoldo Aleman, once again wins, but the Sandinistas hold a significant block of seats in the legislature.

Lakes and Rivers,
Earthquakes and Volcanoes

Nicaragua is located almost exactly in the center of Central America. Honduras borders it to the north, and Costa Rica to the south. Nicaragua is not large. Its area is 50,464 square miles (130,700 square kilometers) with a population, in 1995, of four million. Its coasts face the Pacific Ocean on one side and the Caribbean Sea, towards the Atlantic, on the other. Large lake areas which lie towards the Pacific coast total 4,500 square miles (11,655 square kilometers) with Lake Nicaragua by far the largest. The river network makes Nicaragua ideal for a canal joining the Pacific and Atlantic oceans.

Nicaragua may be separated into three regions: the highly fertile Pacific region; the wetter and cooler Central Highlands; and the hot and humid Atlantic coast.

The west of the country contains the major towns and cities including the capital of Nicaragua, Managua. Also in this region, there are many young volcanoes, some still active, which stretch from the Gulf of Fonseca to Lake Nicaragua.

The lakes of Nicaragua are the largest freshwater lakes in Central America. Lake Nicaragua is 100 miles (161 kilometers) long by 47 miles (75 kilometers) wide; Lake Managua 35 miles (56 kilometers) long and 15 miles (24 kilometers) wide. They are joined by the Tipitapa River. Lake Nicaragua drains into the San Juan River, which forms the boundary between Nicaragua and Costa Rica, and flows into the Caribbean Sea. From the southeast edge of Lake Nicaragua, it is just 12 miles (19 kilometers) to the Pacific Ocean—hence the suitability of Nicaragua as a site for a Pacific-Atlantic canal.

The west of Nicaragua is liable to suffer earthquakes, which have flattened Managua twice, in 1931 and 1972, and also to volcanic eruptions. Yet the volcanoes have a positive side. Their periodic eruptions and scatterings of ash have made the Pacific plains area a highly fertile agricultural region.

A spectacular example of the effects of the earthquake which struck Managua in 1972, causing terrible destruction. This building has been concertina'd to half its original height.

This is how Nicaragua's most recent serious earthquake was reported in the press.

THOUSANDS DEAD AS EARTHQUAKES STRIKE NICARAGUAN CITY
Mexico City, December 23rd

A series of powerful earthquakes destroyed a large part of the Nicaraguan capital of Managua early today, crumpling buildings and sparking fires that killed or injured tens of thousands of persons.

Reports from neighboring Costa Rica said the Nicaraguan Health Ministry estimated that at least 18,000 persons had been killed by collapsing buildings or fires that followed. An additional 40,000 persons were injured and 200,000 left homeless. The city has a population of 325,000.

Pilots who flew over Managua said as much as seventy percent of the city was in ruins. Fires started by the earthquake burned out of control. The water supply was cut off and there was no water for fire fighting or for drinking. Electricity was also knocked out.

Managua, a former Indian village on whose site the Spanish conquistadors founded a city in the sixteenth century, has been repeatedly stricken by disaster. In addition to the earthquakes of 1885 and 1931, the latter recording six on the Richter scale, the city was ruined by floodwaters from Lake Managua in 1876, was heavily damaged when an arsenal exploded in 1902 and was devastated by civil war in 1912.

The city of Managua eighteen months after the 1972 earthquake—little progress has been made in the task of rebuilding.

Among the buildings demolished by the quakes were the Presidential Palace; the cathedral; the newspaper offices of *La Prensa* and *Novedades*; the United States Embassy; two of the city's three major hotels and the Gran Hotel; and all the public utility offices. Most of the other buildings and houses were either destroyed or heavily damaged.

New York Times,
December 24, 1972

The Central Highlands, northeast of the lakes, is a less fertile region. The high, wooded peaks which reach about 3,000-6,000 feet (900-1,800 meters) are only sparsely populated by farmers and communities of Indians.

The east, which makes up 56 percent of the land area of Nicaragua, is lowland called La Mosquitia, or the Miskito (Mosquito) coast. Hot and humid, the soil is not highly fertile and, as a result, the area is not densely populated. Only close to the rivers like the Escondido, the Grande, the Prinzapolka and the Coco, is there fertile soil.

The Atlantic coast is the wettest area of Nicaragua with 100-250 inches (254-636 centimeters) of rain annually. The western slopes of the Central Highlands and the Pacific coast are less wet with annual rainfall of about 40-60 inches (100-150 centimeters). May to October is generally reckoned to be the rainy season; December to April the dry period. Like the rest of the Caribbean, Nicaragua suffers from hurricanes in the months of July to October.

Nicaragua has a barely adequate transportation system. Roads vary from the Pan-American Highway which enters and leaves from Costa Rica and Honduras, to minor tracks which may be washed away in the rainy season. Nicaragua had no roads to speak of until the Second World War, and the country has much work to do to improve its roadways. The 214 miles (344 kilometers) of railroads in Nicaragua are largely unused due to the age and condition of the track and rolling stock. The government has plans to renovate the railroad system and improve communications. Navigable rivers, especially in the east

Nicaragua has many mines like this one. Iron ore, gold and silver are still mined today.

of the country, add to the choice of transportation. Buses, even trucks converted into buses, are the main means of getting around.

Most visitors to Nicaragua land at the Augusto Cesar Sandino Airport at Managua. There are several other minor airports throughout the country. The major ports are Corinto, Puerto Sandino (which used to be called Puerto Somoza) and Bluefields, effectively covering all regions, with several minor ports functioning in the coastal export and import trades.

Gold and silver were mined in Nicaragua by the Spaniards and are still mined today though in much smaller quantities. Nicaragua's wealth would appear to lie in its rich and varied agriculture where possibilities for growth and development exist.

18

The country is not over-populated and there are agricultural areas which could be more effectively used.

Nicaragua has been a poor country throughout most of its history. Today it is struggling out of the poverty and underdevelopment which have resulted from its colonization and unequal relationship with the rest of the world. From the nineteenth century, Nicaragua has had a close, though not always beneficial, relationship with the United States. Such a relationship goes some way to explaining the United States' hostility towards Nicaragua after its revolution in 1979.

Managua became the capital of Nicaragua almost by accident. Out of the competition and hostility that existed between León, the old capital, and Granada, Managua rose to prominence as a compromise between the two. However, as it is a compromise,

A luxurious modern building in Managua, in stark contrast to some of the capital's poorer sections.

Managua is far from being the best location for the nation's capital. Just 150 feet (46 meters) above sea level and 20 miles (32 kilometers) away from the coast, it is a very hot city. Lake Managua provides no cooling breezes, but just seems to add to the city's heat and humidity. There is also the fact that Managua is built upon a geological fault line, leaving it prone to earthquakes that have devastated it on numerous occasions. Although the last of the Somozas pledged himself "to rebuild Managua," the center of the city is still lacking buildings and the construction of these is yet one more task for the post-Sandinista government to add to its list of priorities.

Close to the capital, on the shore of Lake Managua, are *Las Huellas de Acahualinca* (the footsteps of Acahualinca) which represent something of a mystery. Thousands of years old, and perfectly preserved in rock near the lake, are the visible footprints of at least seventeen men and women, running towards the lake shore. They are criss-crossed by the hoof marks of a deer, and the prints of a tiger and other animals. Why? Could they have been fleeing from a volcanic eruption from one of Nicaragua's still-active volcanoes? Were they fleeing from something else? The women's footprints sank deeper into the mud than those of the men. Were they carrying the children, or some of their worldly possessions? One of the men's feet sank even deeper. Was he carrying a friend? His wife? We could guess forever. The footprints of Acahualinca are a unique picture from very early Nicaraguan history that will continue to puzzle,

The volcano at Masaya—one of the many volcanoes throughout Nicaragua, some of which are still active.

perhaps for as long as the prints have already been there.

Close to Managua is León Viejo (Old León) at the base of the Momotombo volcano. This was the original capital of Nicaragua, founded in 1524. But when it was destroyed in an earthquake in 1610, the city was moved to its present site. Archaeologists are excavating this ancient city which is slowly giving up its treasures and providing an intriguing picture of what life was like in the early years of Spanish rule.

Momotombo volcano, 4,000 feet (1,220 meters) high, is still active and smoke can often be seen rising from its crater. Momotombito (Little Momotombo) rises up from the waters of

Lake Managua. Tipitapa, just 12 miles (19 kilometers) from Managua, is famous for its hot springs. The scalding-hot water, heated by volcanic activity, has to be cooled before it can be used as spa-water which has special healing properties. Tipitapa is famous, too, for quapote, a *pescado sin espinas* (fish without bones) that has been described as "the best fish in the world."

The largest city after Managua is León, 55 miles (89 kilometers) northwest of the capital. Leon was the capital for three hundred years, until Managua took on the honor in 1858, and it still has all the imposing grace of an important city. Its cathedral is the largest in Central America. It is said to have been built in error, when plans for the cathedral of Lima, in Peru, and for a modest church in León got mixed up during the journey

The cathedral in León.

A photograph taken on an *hacienda* (ranch) at harvest time. Oxen are used to help transport the sugarcane.

from Spain. It took a hundred years to build and is an imposing piece of architecture. The cathedral has many interesting features but most Nicaraguans will tell you that it is famous because the poet, Ruben Dario, is buried there. The house in which he lived is a museum in the city. There are many churches more ancient than the cathedral in León. The oldest dates from 1530, not long after the Spaniards established a colony in Nicaragua. Bartholomé de las Casas, the champion of the Indian peoples of Latin America, preached there many times.

Close to León is Chinandega, an agricultural center, which processes the cotton, bananas and sugarcane grown in the region.

23

On the coast, some 12 miles (19 kilometers) away is the port of Corinto, through which a large proportion of Nicaragua's exports and imports pass.

Matagalpa is famous as a cattle and coffee town and for some attractive colonial architecture left by the Spaniards. In the nearby Rio Viejo (Old River) Valley, is a wealth of animal and plant life. Lake Apanás is full of fish; in the nearby forest live jaguars, pumas, wild boars, tapirs, sloths and many varieties of monkeys, along with deer and brightly-colored parrots. Here too, lives the rare quetzal bird, the holy bird of the Maya Indians. It has long emerald green tail feathers and a bright red breast.

Hand-rolling cigars in a factory at Estelí—the "tobacco center" of Nicaragua where many Cuban tobacco-growers are now established.

A scene reminiscent of days gone by in Granada, Nicaragua's oldest colonial city.

The city of Estelí, also close to Matagalpa, is famous for its tobacco. Called the "tobacco center" of Central America, its soil and climate are similar to the best tobacco-growing regions in Cuba. In fact many Cuban tobacco-growers moved to Estelí after the Cuban revolution. Today, in Estelí, you can see cigars being rolled by hand with all the skill and care that goes into the manufacture of the world's finest cigars.

Granada, Nicaragua's third city, is the oldest Spanish colonial city. It was founded in 1524 and is set on the shores of Lake Nicaragua at the foot of the Mombacho volcano. The periodic scattering of volcanic ash from the volcano has made this area one of the richest agricultural regions in the country where

25

sugarcane, indigo and cacao are still grown. It has had a vivid history, being sacked several times by pirates, like Henry Morgan and Francis Drake, who traveled to the city from the Caribbean Sea. William Walker made his unsuccessful stand against the other Central American republics from Granada, setting fire to the city on his retreat and leaving behind a flag with the inscription: *Aqui fue Granada–Here was Granada*. Fortunately, Walker did not have his wish and much of the Spanish colonial architecture stands to the present day.

In Lake Nicaragua is an archipelago of over three hundred small, and not so small, islands where once only the wealthy of Nicaragua could afford to go. The lake is full of freshwater sharks that come down Nicaragua's rivers to feast on the abundance of fish, like the quapote. The Isla de Ometepe is the largest of the lake's islands, with two volcanoes, Madera and Concepción. The latter rises to over 5,000 feet (1,610 meters).

From Granada, one can travel by boat to the town of San Carlos at the southeastern end of the lake, where the lake joins the San Juan River. From San Carlos, boats travel to San Juan del Norte on the Caribbean coast. The San Juan River, stretching 120 miles (193 kilometers) represents the border between Nicaragua and Costa Rica and is full of turtles, alligators, sharks and tarpons. Its banks provide a home for the varieties of monkeys, sloths and birds for which Central America is famous.

An interesting geographical feature off the Atlantic (Caribbean) coast of Nicaragua are the Islas del Maiz (Corn Islands). These are 40 miles (64 kilometers) offshore from Bluefields and seem to have been untouched by the passage of time. They are quiet, unspoiled and beautiful islands, populated by Nicaraguans of West Indian descent brought there by the British. Hence, they speak English. The people here are relaxed and friendly and go out of their way to make any traveler's visit memorable.

2

"The Perfectly Happy Province of Nicaragua"

In 1522 or 23 this tyrant (a Spanish explorer called Gil Gonzalez de Avila) went off to the perfectly happy province of Nicaragua and subjugated its people to so much evil, butchery, cruelty, bondage and injustice that no human tongue would be able to describe it. Today (1542) there must be four or five thousand persons in the whole of Nicaragua. The Spaniards kill more every day through the services they extract and the daily personal oppression they exercise. And this, as we have said, used to be one of the most highly populated provinces in the world.

This was the account of the fate of Nicaraguans from the Pacific plains by Bartholomé de las Casas, a Catholic priest, who took up the Indians' cause all over Latin America. His account, and those of other Spanish writers of the time, shows how the original Indian population of Nicaragua was reduced from about a million to just tens of thousands, within a few decades of the arrival on Nicaraguan soil of Gil Gonzalez de Avila.

Although many Indians died in battles against the Spaniards,

Bartholomé de las Casas, a Catholic priest who took up the Indian's cause during the years of Spanish oppression.

this was not the main reason for their decline in numbers. Much more disastrous was the effect of the diseases brought to the New World—the term by which the Spaniards knew Latin America—by the Spaniards themselves. Influenza and measles, minor illnesses today, at least in developed countries, were devastating to a people who had never come into contact with them before. Hundreds of thousands of Nicaraguan Indians died of such diseases within a few years of their "discovery" by the Spaniards.

Slavery was another cause of the dramatic decline in the population. Four to five hundred thousand slaves were captured in the first twenty years of Spanish rule alone. Slave ships took

29

the Nicaraguans to other parts of the Spanish Empire in the Americas. One destination was Peru, where, especially in the 1530s, slaves were brutally used in the gold and silver mines. Slaves were either captured by the Spaniards themselves or handed over by "friendly" Indian chiefs. For them, life was short; perhaps as many as half died while on the slave ships. Those who did arrive at their destination were worked to death in the mines. Not many lasted more than a few years.

The Spaniards came to Nicaragua for the same reasons they entered the other countries in the New World: they wanted to "save" the souls of the Indians. But, and perhaps more importantly, they were also searching for gold and other riches. Many thousands were "saved" in Nicaragua, and ninety thousand pesos' worth of gold sent home, but the expedition proved to be a difficult one for the Spaniards. Not all the Indians were docile and it was only the Pacific plains area that the Spaniards were able to call their own. This was the richest and most densely populated region, inhabited by the Chorotek Indians of the Aztec family. The jungles of the mountains in the northeast, the impenetrable forests of the east and the Atlantic coast region—called the Miskito, or sometimes the Mosquito Coast—where the majority of the Indians lived, were never controlled by the Spaniards. Even during that first exploration by Gil Gonzalez de Avila, the going was far from easy. After making what appeared to be friendly contacts, the Spaniards suffered a surprise attack by several thousand Indians, led by a chief called Dirangien. They had to fall back to the coast where they were set upon by yet more Indians, this time led by Chief Nicarao. Two years later, in another expedition led by Francisco Hernandez de Cordoba, the Spaniards were able to take control of the Pacific coast region. In the rest of Nicaragua, Indians maintained their traditional lifestyle until the end of the nineteenth century.

In the seventeenth century, other European powers were taking an interest in Central America and the Caribbean. From around 1650, the British began to control much of the Caribbean coast. In the 1660s British wood-cutters settled in Belize (named after the British pirate Peter Wallace whose name was changed to Ballace and then Belize) and made a hard living from cutting down and selling *campeche* (logwood) for the dyeing industry. The country became an important base for pirating. Another famous British pirate, Henry Morgan, sacked Panama City in 1671,

A contemporary artist's impression of the sacking of Panama City, by the pirate Henry Morgan, in 1671.

driving the Spaniards further along the coast. By the end of the century, the British were an important force in Central America and the Caribbean. Operating out of Nicaragua's Mosquito Coast, they added slave-hunting to their list of crimes in the region. Along the Mosquito Coast the British made friends with the local Indians and set up bases from which they could engage in smuggling, as well as attack the Spanish settlements. To the present day, the people of the Atlantic coast speak "Coastal English" even though the region was integrated with the rest of the country in 1894. Belize, a near neighbor of Nicaragua, still retains its British connection.

Nicaraguans benefited little from their links with Spain. The country was treated by the Spaniards merely as a source of slaves, with captured Nicaraguans being sent to Chile, Ecuador, Panama, Peru and Santo Domingo. To those places, and to other Spanish colonies, were exported leather and dried meat, wood, cocoa, and dye-stuffs. When there were no more people to take into slavery, the country became a poor backwater of the Spanish Empire, existing only for the benefit of the rich Spanish landowners in Granada on the north shores of Lake Nicaragua and the merchants of León in the northeast.

Great rivalry developed between these two centers. As Granada was thought to be the future administrative center of Nicaragua, it was settled by the more aristocratic Spaniards. Soldiers and those of the lower classes were sent to León. But it was León which became the center of the country and the people of Granada had to accept the rule of a number of corrupt

32

administrators whom they considered below them in rank. The Granadese wealth came mainly from cattle-raising. The Leonese got theirs from shipbuilding, wood crafts, and from service to the government, which added a further source of friction. After independence, the friction between the two cities boiled over into civil war.

Nicaragua won its independence from Spain in stages. First it became a part of the Mexican Empire in 1822, then a part of the Central America Federation in 1823, and finally a sovereign state in 1838. There was little advantage to most Nicaraguans from independence. Under Spanish control, large estates, called *haciendas*, were established where Indians and *mestizos* (of mixed Indian and Spanish descent) were forced to

A *mestizo* woman. Much of the country's population today is of mixed Spanish and American Indian origin.

work. Some Indians and *mestizos* lived on *chacras*, small family plots. Independence brought an end to slavery in 1824 and forced labor gradually disappeared at the end of the nineteenth century. However, the memory of slavery and forced labor was to remain until recent times.

With the Spaniards gone, the rivalries between León and Granada ran unchecked. In 1811, even before the end of Spanish rule, León led Granada into a revolt against Spain, only to change its position, leaving the Granadese at the mercy of Spain's revenge. After that, the two cities were constantly and literally at one another's throats. The Leónese came to be known as Liberals for their admiration of the French and American revolutions, the Granadese as Conservatives for holding on to traditional, aristocratic ideas. Once Nicaragua became a sovereign nation, the two rival camps fought for control of the country. Presidents came and went; the country fell into a greater state of chaos and instability. Other nations, which had always looked at Nicaragua with great interest, now began to interfere in its affairs.

When Alexander von Humboldt, the famous German scientist, traveled throughout Spanish America in the late eighteenth/early nineteenth century, he concluded that a canal connecting the Atlantic and Pacific Oceans was practicable at five points, but that the isthmus of Nicaragua and that of Cupica (now known as Darién) was by far the best site. The Spaniards had progressed no further than making surveys for the construction of a canal. In the nineteenth century, especially in the 1840s when the United States expanded to the Pacific coast and gold was discovered in California, considerable U.S. interest developed in Nicaragua as the location for an inter-oceanic route. Gold hunters traveled through Nicaragua on their way to the Californian gold fields. The route through that country was quicker and safer than others in Central America. The Panama route, for example, held many dangers, not least the fevers that could be caught from the swarms of mosquitoes. In 1850, continued rivalry between the United States and Britain resulted in the Clayton-Bulwer Treaty in which the two countries pledged not to colonize Central America or to gain an unfair advantage in relation to a Pacific-Atlantic canal. The treaty did not bring peace to Nicaragua as the British and North Americans took sides in the dispute in pursuit of their own interests. The British supported the Conservatives, the Americans the Liberals.

It was the Liberals who enlisted the help of an American named William Walker. In 1855 he sailed to Nicaragua with a group of mercenaries and eventually took the city of Granada. Before very long Walker had set himself up as "elected" president of Nicaragua. His "presidency" was recognized by the president of the United States. Walker deemed that English should be the country's official language, and he reinstituted slavery, hoping that this action would give support to the Southern states of the United States in their fight against the abolitionists (those who wanted slavery abolished) in the North. Walker's flag bore the motto: "Five or None!" for he had dreams of taking over the

Precious metals, so important to the Spaniards, are still to be found in Nicaragua today. These people are panning for gold.

whole of Central America. This was his undoing, for the five Central American states of the time would have none of this interference in their affairs. Troops were dispatched to Nicaragua in 1857 and Walker was forced to flee to the United States. Unable to give up his dream, he returned to Central America four years later to try to renew his "presidency." However, after taking the town of Trujillo in Honduras, he was captured by the British Navy, handed over to the Honduran government and executed. Nicaraguans (Nicas) celebrate September 14th in commemoration of the battle of San Jacinto against Walker's mercenaries. After Walker's defeat, the two rival sides in Nicaragua settled their differences. The Conservatives ruled the country in relative peace and stability for the next twenty years.

36

Several thousand Indians were killed in 1881 in the War of the *Comuneros* (tenant farmers), defending their lands from rich landowners who wanted to add to their coffee estates. This was the beginning of Nicaragua's coffee era, and Managua, the capital from 1852, grew as a result of the boom. Coffee became the most important export until the 1950s and 1960s when cotton took over.

Coffee brought power to the rich landowners who produced it. In 1893 the Conservatives were displaced by a Liberal, Jose Santos Zelaya, later described by the U.S. president, William Howard Taft, as a "blot on the history of Nicaragua." Zelaya was a dictator, but he was neither a harsh nor a cruel leader. During his sixteen years in power, Zelaya initiated many reforms; new schools were opened, new lands offered for the growing coffee industry, new roads and telegraph lines built. Exports of coffee, bananas, timber and gold all increased. In 1894, Zelaya sent troops to Bluefields on the Mosquito Coast, accepted the Miskito Indian chief's request for incorporation with the rest of Nicaragua, and expelled the British Consul. Zelaya also worked to bring the other countries of Central America together as a confederation called the *Republica Major* (Greater Republic) but without lasting success.

It was tension between the United States and Zelaya that finally brought him down. An inter-ocean canal that would have given the United States rights over Nicaraguan territory was unacceptable to Zelaya. The United States engineered events in Panama so as to build a canal there. When it became known that

Zelaya was in discussion with the British and Japanese to build a rival canal, the United States indicated that they would like a new president to replace him.

A Conservative revolt broke out in Bluefields and Zelaya was forced into resignation and exile. The new government, and the one which rapidly followed, did little for Nicaragua, resulting in a rebellion led by Benjamin Zeledon to rid Nicaragua of "the traitor to the Fatherland." Out of fear that the rebels would win, U.S. Marines were sent into Nicaragua. Zeledon was captured and killed, and his body dragged through the streets before he was buried. One of the onlookers at this unpleasant spectacle, which had made his "blood boil with rage," was a young boy, Augusto Cesar Sandino. He was to play a dramatic part in Nicaragua's struggle for independence.

3

The United States, Sandino and the Somoza Family

United States Marines were stationed on Nicaraguan soil from 1912 to 1925 and again from 1926 to 1933. United States policy-makers apparently felt that it was necessary to ensure a friendly government in Nicaragua (friendly to the United States), since that country was in the middle of Central America and faced the Caribbean—both areas considered the "back-yard" of the United States. There was little benefit to Nicaragua from the two occupations by United States troops. The second occupation was important, however, as it saw the beginnings of the Somoza family's dictatorship of Nicaragua, and the rebirth of revolutionary ideas—ideas which would for a time triumph in Nicaragua and set that country along a radically different path from its neighbors in Central America.

The revolution was kept going by Augusto Cesar Sandino who led a long guerrilla struggle against the government's injustices and the United States' occupation of his country. In his early years, Sandino knew what it meant to be poor, even going to the debtor's prison with his mother at the age of nine. As a young man his life was shattered when, in a fight, he shot his opponent and was forced to flee the country. He worked in Honduras, Guatemala, and Mexico before returning to Nicaragua. It was a different person who returned. Sandino had experienced the Mexican revolution and had felt the strong anti-American feelings in other countries. He wanted to change things in Nicaragua and immediately joined the rebels fighting the government and the United States occupation forces. In 1927, when the rest of the Liberals had accepted a peace treaty, Sandino continued with the fight. He had a force of three hundred men, all of them well-armed and disciplined, and he vowed to continue fighting until the last American soldier had left Nicaragua. At first the methods of warfare he used were conventional. Large numbers of his men would attack the enemy, well established in their own positions. As many of his troops were lost in the fighting, Sandino changed his tactics to hit and run. He attracted the support of the *campesinos* (country people) with whom he and his troops lived and who warned him of any enemy approaches. This resulted in a war which U.S. and government troops were unable to win. The bombardment of towns and the forced relocation of whole villages made Sandino's cause even more popular. Even when U.S. troops left in 1933, Sandino was still a force to be reckoned with. Accepting peace terms offered by the new President Sacasa, Sandino's men laid down their arms. Sandino himself refused offers of high office

40

This imposing portrait of Augusto Cesar Sandino, founder of the revolutionary movement which bore his name, was hung outside the cathedral in Managua.

from the government, preferring to devote his energies to setting up peasant co-operative farms which, he believed, would open up a new future for Nicaragua.

But there were other stirrings in Nicaragua. The National Guard, set up by the Americans in 1927 and led by Anastasio Somoza Garcia, saw the very existence of Sandino as a threat. On February 21, 1934, Sandino was invited to a banquet at the Presidential Palace in Managua. That evening he was shot down in cold blood by Somoza's National Guard. Stripped of its leader, the movement which had been led by Sandino, was unable to regroup itself. In 1936 Anastasio Somoza took power for himself, beginning nearly fifty years of misery for the

Nicaraguan people which only came to an end with the successful Sandinista revolution of 1979.

Within twenty years, Somoza was to be the richest person in Central America. As president of Nicaragua he was able to enrich himself at the country's expense. Within eight years of becoming president, Somoza was Nicaragua's largest landowner and coffee producer. Before taking office he had no wealth of his own. Soon there was no part of Nicaraguan business in which Somoza did not have an interest. By 1979 the Somoza family fortune totalled U.S. $150 million.

In his nineteen years as dictator, Somoza kept himself in power through his control of the National Guard. He kept the guard loyal to him by encouraging them to be as corrupt as he was himself. Somoza also stayed on good terms with the United States. The United States' enemies were Somoza's enemies. In return, United States governments supported Somoza and his rule by the National Guard. The rich Nicaraguans became even richer under Somoza. However, there was little improvement in the condition of life for the ordinary people.

Somoza's dictatorship, and his life, came to an abrupt end in 1956 when a young poet, Rigoberto Lopez Perez, evaded the security at a reception for Somoza and shot the dictator five times. In a letter to his mother, Lopez Perez said: "What I have done is a duty any Nicaraguan who truly loves his country should have done a long time ago." But this was not to be the end of Somoza rule. Luis, the older of Anastasio's two sons, became president and continued in power until 1963.

Luis Somoza Debayle had a softer approach than his father. Social reforms, like housing programs, education, social security, and limited land reform all came into being during Luis Somoza's presidency. However, they were mainly for show. The lives of poor Nicaraguans were no better under this Somoza; elections were still unfair and the National Guard still ruled the country. Attempts were made, no doubt following the example of the successful revolution in Cuba, to overthrow Somoza. The Sandinista Front for National Liberation, known as the FSLN, came into prominence. A third Somoza, Anastasio, became president in 1967 in another dishonest election. Like his father, whose name he shared, Anastasio Somoza preferred harsher methods of rule than his brother. The power and presence of the

General Anastasio Somoza, the third member of the Somoza family to take power. He ruled Nicaragua from 1967-1979.

National Guard once again became the daily reality of Nicaragua. The government became increasingly corrupt and inefficient. The Somoza family fortunes increased. However, the 1970s were to bring crisis after crisis for Somoza, eventually leading to his defeat and exile from Nicaragua.

The first obvious signs of discontent came after the 1972 earthquake, which killed ten thousand people, and razed to the ground a large part of Managua, the capital. Somoza took relief funds from abroad for his own use. The center of the capital was never rebuilt despite vast resources being given for that purpose. Instead, the National Guard officers built themselves luxury homes. The poor who had lost their houses, and often their families as well, in the earthquake, were forced to make do with

A Somoza supporter participating in a rally in León, preceding the 1974 election in which Somoza retained power.

Children outside the wooden shacks in which they lived. These were put up as temporary accommodation, after the earthquake of 1972 destroyed many homes.

wooden shacks. Strikes and demonstrations against Somoza became common. More and more young people began to join the FSLN. All sections of society in Nicaragua, including the Catholic Church, began to question Somoza's rule.

On August 20, 1975 Edgard Lang Sacaso, son of a wealthy Nicaraguan family close to President Anastasio Somoza, left home to join the guerrillas of the FSLN. When he was killed in April 1979, in a battle against the National Guard in León,

45

his father published in the *New York Times* the letter he had left behind for his family.

> *I'm sure that in recent months you have noticed my somewhat strange behavior. I no longer go to parties, I appear and disappear.*
>
> *This is because, my dear parents, I am a revolutionary, a member of the Sandinista Liberation Front. I have taken this decision for the following reasons:*
>
> *(1) I have lived, enjoyed life and spent wildly for twenty years while thousands of children, sons of workers and peasants, had considerable hunger and died from malnutrition and lack of medical care, because in our country there is misery and backwardness.*
>
> *(2) The sacred mission of all Nicaraguans is to fight for the liberation of our people. This generation is doing what past generations should have done. You bequeathed to us an enslaved Nicaragua where injustice and crime reign. We do not want our children to make the same accusation of us.*
>
> *(3) We young people can no longer support the foul odor emanating from the Somoza regime. If our parents accustomed themselves to this rotten government, we are prepared to risk our lives to end it.*
>
> *(4) I am going to the mountains because that is where the patriots, the honest men and those who are sacrificing everything for their people, are to be found.*

I want you to know that I am going voluntarily, so forget the idea that someone is using me.

You will say that I am a bad son. But it is quite the contrary.

You wanted me to be an honest man and in Nicaragua, please believe me, one can only be honest in these times fighting with all the forces against the Somoza tyranny of which our people are so tired.

Please don't look for me, or even try to go to the police, because that would seriously endanger my life, since I am not willing to be caught alive.

I send you each a kiss and an embrace and thank you for your effort and sacrifice to make me a good man. Well, these efforts and sacrifices have borne fruit.

I am a revolutionary which is the highest rank to which a human being can ascribe.

I had hoped that our parting would not be painful, but circumstances have so determined. I, like Sandino, would like a "free country or death" and that is why I am going.

Embraces and kisses from your son who loves you more than ever. Until very soon, that is, until the final victory.

Edgard

By 1977 Somoza was in deep trouble. Nicaragua had been identified as the country with the worst human rights record in the whole of Latin America. The president of the United States, Jimmy Carter, began to put pressure on Somoza. The Church in Nicaragua, too, publicly denounced his treatment of the people. The press

47

A rally in support of the FSLN—the Sandinista Front for national Liberation which led the opposition to Somoza rule.

increasingly came to report the worst cases of Somoza's rule. Pedro Chamorro, a journalist who had openly attacked the president in his newspaper, was assassinated on his way to work. The FSLN became an important force against Somoza. National Guard headquarters were attacked; strikes, demonstrations and uprisings became common. Somoza reacted with characteristic brutality. Hundreds of Nicaraguans were killed or "disappeared" from the streets. The FSLN became more daring. In August 1978, twenty-five FSLN guerrillas took over the National Palace, posing as soldiers of the National Guard and held fifteen

48

hundred hostages. Somoza was forced to hand over a huge ransom, give the FSLN the opportunity to broadcast statements against him, and promise safe passage out of the country for FSLN prisoners.

This attack on the National Palace encouraged others to join the FSLN or to begin to stand up to Somoza and the National Guard in other ways. Throughout Nicaragua, the people began to take matters into their own hands, defy the National Guard, and take command of their own towns. With few weapons to hold off the fiercest attacks by the National Guard, many thousands were to lose their lives. Somoza, fighting to hold on to power, attacked any resistance from the air and then sent in his

The National Palace in Managua, stormed by the Sandinistas in 1979. (Note the FSLN banner).

troops to finish the job. The lesson was not lost on the FSLN. If Somoza was to be defeated, a better organized, better equipped force would have to drive him out. This was the task for 1979. The final offensive was announced in June. The end was in sight for Somoza who fled to Miami on July 17th. On July 19th, the FSLN entered Managua and accepted the surrender of what remained of the National Guard. This is how the news was reported in the *New York Times*:

NICARAGUAN REBELS TAKE OVER CAPITAL, ENDING CIVIL WAR. DEFEATED NATIONAL GUARD FORMALLY SURRENDERS–SANDINIST JUNTA IS DUE IN NICARAGUA TODAY
Managua, Nicaragua July 19th

Two days after President Anastasio Somoza Debayle fled Nicaragua, Sandinist rebels took control of Nicaragua today, completing the defeat of the National Guard and ending a seven week old war that left more than ten thousand people dead.

Excited crowds lined the streets of the capital as thousands of young rebels, many of them dressed in olive green uniforms and carrying automatic rifles, drove around the city, waving the red and black Sandinist flag and firing shots into the air.

Some Sandinist units occupied General Somoza's military compound, known as the "bunker" seizing hundreds of weapons and freeing dozens of political prisoners. Two rebel commanders installed themselves in the deposed dictator's office.

Nine miles away, cheering crowds pulled down an equestrian

50

Members of the Sandinista Liberation Army during a break in the fighting against the *Contras*.

statue of the deposed president's father, General Anastasio Somoza Garcia, who founded the Somoza family dynasty more than four decades ago.

A five member provisional *junta*, named by the guerrillas last month to govern the country until elections are held, is expected to arrive here tomorrow for a huge reception. Early yesterday, the *junta* flew from Costa Rica to establish a temporary capital in León, Nicaragua's second largest city, which has been in rebel hands for six weeks. The Sandinist takeover of Managua came suddenly and almost peacefully in the wake of General Somoza's resignation and flight into exile in Miami.

The National Guard's morale was destroyed. With guard

barracks surrendering to the rebels in several cities, the new guard commander decided yesterday to hand over power to the provisional *junta*. Early this morning the Chiefs of Staff abandoned the Somoza "bunker" and reportedly left the country. With most officers going into hiding or seeking asylum in foreign embassies, ordinary soldiers quickly left their posts, many of them discarding their weapons and tearing off their uniforms. Some were already wearing civilian clothes under their uniforms.

New York Times
July 20, 1979

4

Rebuilding the Country

The Government of National Reconstruction, installed by the FSLN, had a formidable task. Fifty thousand people had been killed in the war, one hundred thousand wounded, forty thousand orphaned. A fifth of the population were homeless, a third of the work force without work. Somoza made sure, before he left, that whoever took over from him would face staggering difficulties. There was nothing to show for the huge loans Somoza had taken from foreign banks; most had gone to Miami with him. Industry and commerce had been destroyed in air raids in a final act of revenge. The country was almost bankrupt, owing $1.6 billion to foreign banks, the highest per capita debt (national debt in relation to the size of the population) in Latin America.

In 1979, the first year of the revolution, all Nicaraguan earnings from exports would only have paid the interest on the debt. The major towns had been destroyed or damaged in the bombings. Three quarters of the land, particularly that of the

Nicaraguans involved in rebuilding work—very necessary after the destruction caused by the war.

cotton and sugar plantations, had not been sown because of the war. What the government proposed was a combined effort by all Nicaraguans to rebuild the country.

Many new public works were begun. New parks, roads and recreation centers were built, providing jobs for the thousands of unemployed. In 1980 a massive Literacy Campaign was begun. Many vaccination programs were started. Doctors and nurses were trained in order to provide health care for poor Nicaraguans who had never experienced health care before.

The Government of National Reconstruction consisted of a majority from the FSLN but included members of other political parties along with representatives from business, and from the Catholic Church which had played an important part in the struggle against Somoza. The FSLN was the most important political force in Nicaragua. The red and black flag of the Sandinistas was visible everywhere. Sandinista organizations grew in number in 1979. The CDS's—Sandinista Defence Committees—were organized in every neighborhood or village in the country. Their task was to be the "eyes and ears" of the revolution; and to aid the economic and social drives of the government. A Sandinista Youth Organization was formed, along with a trade union umbrella organization called the Sandinista Workers' Control (CST). The women of the revolution, who had fought to ensure victory over Somoza, had their own organization in the Luisa Armanda Espinosa Association of Nicaraguan Women (AMNLAE). The FSLN began to publish their own daily newspaper *Barricada* and to run their own radio and television station. The Sandinist Popular Army, the Sandinist Police, and the Sandinist Peoples Militia gave the FSLN military control of the country.

The FSLN and the government were determined to create a new revolutionary Nicaragua that would be entirely different from what had gone before and which would ensure Nicaragua's social and economic well-being. The death penalty was banned, though there were some examples of the people taking the law into their own hands and settling accounts. Several thousand members of the National Guard, who had been arrested after the Sandinistas' victory, were either released or tried before special courts. Thirty-year jail sentences were the maximum that any were given.

Members of the Sandinista army wearing black and red scarves—in imitation of their country's flag.

The press was given its freedom and there reappeared newspapers which represented different political parties and interests. Political parties were given the right to exist and to organize, for the FSLN saw Nicaragua's future as a system of democracy like that in North America or Europe. Elections were promised as soon as practicable.

The FSLN's position with regard to the United States was a very realistic one. Nicaragua is a small country, very close to the most powerful country in the world. Nicaragua needs to be able to sell its exports to the United States and to have friendly relations but it cannot afford to be dominated by the United States as it was in the past. So the FSLN determined to continue its friendly relations with other revolutionary regimes—of which the United States disapproved—such as Cuba and Vietnam.

What the Nicaraguans hoped to show by their revolution was that it was *different* from all the others. They did not want to be seen as a "second Cuba" or "another Chile" or "another Grenada." Their revolution was not a pale reflection, nor an imitation of any other. The involvement of the Catholic Church and the high degree of participation by women set their revolution apart. But, as the government was to point out many times, winning the struggle against Somoza was the easy part. Actually making the revolution work was to be much more difficult.

5

Industry and Agriculture

When the Spaniards landed on Nicaraguan soil they discovered, as they had elsewhere in the New World, a well-established, even prosperous, society. The Indian tribes, descendants of Mayans and Aztecs from the north, lived in villages of a few hundred to cities of tens of thousands. Chiefs headed the tribes, expecting loyalty from their followers. The lives of Nicaragua's Indians were based upon agriculture. Each Indian had a claim to a piece of land that was owned by the tribe as a whole. The fertile soil produced a range of crops: maize, cassava, beans, tobacco and plenty of vegetables. The Indians' diet was certainly superior to that of the Spaniards who came to "civilize" them. Markets in the different regions added to the variety of goods available and made communication and contact between the regions possible.

From the moment the Spaniards arrived, the Indians' way of life was doomed. The Spaniards wanted gold, not agricultural produce, and when the gold ran out they took slaves. With the

Cowboys with part of their herd on a big *hacienda* near Granada. Beef is an important export for Nicaragua.

effect of the diseases imported from Europe, the population withered and with it the Indians' agriculture. Some agriculture continued under Spanish rule but most lands returned to jungle. Cattle-raising, which required less labor, produced hides, dried and salted meats, and tallow for other Spanish colonies. Nor did the economy develop much immediately after independence, although the number of small, self-sufficient farms, or *huertas* did increase.

It was coffee which changed Nicaragua's economy, and with it the whole society of the country. Coffee had been grown in the 1840s and in the 1850s and was being enjoyed by travelers passing through Nicaragua on their way to California. By the 1870s it was well on the way to being Nicaragua's sole export crop. The production of one crop by a country is known as monoculture and can have very harmful effects. The 1870s and 1880s saw more and more land taken over for coffee. Indians lost the right to their ancient heritage and as many as five thousand were killed in battles to wrest their lands from them.

Coffee did not offer year-round work. The harvest lasts from November to February after which there is unemployment in the *tiempo muerto* (dead season). But this was the only work there was for the country people of Nicaragua. The large landowners were

Coffee cherries growing. Coffee beans are actually the seeds in the center of each cherry.

Workers on a Nicaraguan coffee plantation. Coffee is one of the country's most important crops.

those who profited from coffee but even for them there were ups and downs depending on whether the world wanted to buy coffee or not. Coffee remained Nicaragua's most important export until the 1950s.

In the 1950s and 1960s other crops were raised and new products manufactured but life for most Nicaraguans remained dismal. Besides coffee, Nicaragua now started exporting beef, cotton, bananas, sugar, wood and seafood. But cotton was by far the most important new product; in 1949, 379 tons were exported, by 1955 this figure had risen to 43,971 tons. Soon,

61

eighty percent of the land by the Pacific coast had been turned over to cotton.

The 1960s were times of optimism for Nicaragua. The United States offered, through its "Alliance for Progress" plan, aid and assistance to develop the economy. The Central America Common Market, which came into existence in 1960, offered opportunities for the Central American countries to work together. By the early 1970s, however, optimism had evaporated. The Somozas pushed aside those with the skills and commitment to contribute to Nicaragua's economic development, preferring instead to work through the corrupt National Guard officers with whom they effectively controlled the country.

Austerity

Our country has many debts. It is broke.
Many citizens are unemployed.
We don't have many crops.
Somocism (the Somozas) is to blame for all of this.
In spite of these conditions, we can improve the economy.
With more dedication, we will increase the country's resources.
We are sharing what little the Somocistas left.
Austerity is necessary.

From the 1980 Literacy Workbook
"Dawn of the People"

Small wonder that Nicaragua was an undeveloped country on the eve of the Sandinista revolution, with the mass of the people impoverished and suffering great hardship.

The Sandinistas, from 1979, were committed to change all that. Their policies were designed to make possible a "just, free, and fraternal human life in our fatherland." But if this policy was to bring change, the center of attention would have to move from the privileged few to the majority of Nicaraguans who, in the past, had been the ones to suffer from the corruption and inefficiency of the Somozas.

One of the government's first acts was to recover what was recoverable from the Somozas. Much of the wealth they had obtained from Nicaragua had been spirited out of the country, but the farms, industries and real estate remaining were taken over and nationalized by the government. Banks and insurance companies were also taken over by the government to deal with the urgent task of reconstruction following the war that had been waged against Somoza.

Private business and farms continued to operate under the new government but only as long as they were run in the public interest. If land was not used efficiently, it was confiscated by the state. Businesses had to contribute more to society through taxes. On the other hand, the government made grants and loans to private companies to enable them to rebuild and recover after the war.

The new government also had the task of dealing with the debt of $1.6 billion left by Somoza and making sure that, in the future,

Bread being made at a workers' collective.

Nicaragua did not get into a similar position. To this end, Nicaragua established contacts with many new trading partners. A number of countries offered aid and loans to the new government. The United States government of President Ronald Reagan, however, became increasingly concerned that Nicaragua was coming under communist influence.

6

The Literacy Campaign

When Nicaragua's revolution began, in 1979, over half the population were illiterate, that is to say, unable to read or write. To deal once and for all with this problem, a National Literacy Campaign was begun the next year. Other countries had had literacy campaigns; Mexico in the 1920s, Guinea-Bissau and Mozambique in the 1970s, Cuba in 1961. The Nicaraguans had plenty of experience to draw from.

1980 was the Year of Literacy and the whole country was caught up in the campaign in one way or another. Teachers were taught, books were printed, all the materials necessary for a campaign like this—which had a distinctly military flavor—were produced. Everything was done to make sure the campaign was successful. From March to August 1980, brigades of more than a hundred thousand volunteers went to battle against the "enemy"—illiteracy.

Most of the volunteers, called *brigadistas*, were young people. Sixty thousand of them were out in the countryside, living and working alongside the *campesinos* (country people) they had gone to teach to read and write. Just as in the Literacy Campaign in Cuba, many of the *brigadistas* felt that, by the end of the campaign, they had learned more than the *campesinos* they had gone to teach. Most had never had very much contact with the rural areas of the country and certainly had no idea of the hardship suffered by the people who lived there. Life for the *campesinos* was hard. Their houses were usually inadequate—without electricity, running water, or toilet facilities. Their work was harsh and unceasing. Naturally, they viewed the teenage *brigadistas* who came to live among them with great suspicion.

It was not long, however, before these suspicions had been worn away by the hard work and dedication of the *brigadistas*. Literacy classes were held on weekends and in the evenings so as not to get in the way of work. Nicaragua, after all, needed every particle of food and raw materials it could produce. For the rest of the time, *brigadistas* worked in the fields alongside the *campesinos*, doing whatever work was necessary. They learned about agriculture by planting and harvesting crops, made handicrafts, looked after cattle and milked cows—all a very long way from their experience of life in the towns and cities.

In Cuba, over thirty years after their Literacy Campaign, ex-*brigadistas* still visit country families they befriended in 1961. In Nicaragua this experience could well be repeated. Close friendships were made between the *campesinos* and the volunteers from the towns. The *campesinos* learned about the lives of the volunteers and vice versa. The *brigadistas* went home determined

A poster publicizing the National Literacy Campaign.

to make life better for those living in the countryside. Some help had already been given, for in addition to teaching basic writing and reading skills, the *brigadistas* had worked on getting rid of malaria, and on the health education program. They had been trained to look out for minerals which could help their country's development, and to note any archaeological remains they came across. They collected plants and insects for later study; learned songs, stories and folk tales from the *campesinos*, and made detailed notes on the economic life of the countryside.

Not everyone in Nicaragua agreed with the campaign, some seeing it as "communist indoctrination." And there were more serious problems to face. In the remote areas of the north and east the *brigadistas* were physically attacked by *Contras* (counter-revolutionaries) who were ex-members of the National Guard, camped in Honduras.

67

Those who attacked the campaign were in a minority, for the great majority of Nicaraguans agreed that if illiteracy continued it would hold back the attempts being made to build a better future for everyone. The Catholic Church was at the forefront of the campaign; in fact, its director was a priest, Father Fernando Cardenal. A massive involvement by the Nicaraguan people and support and money from around the world all contributed to the success of this campaign, which reduced illiteracy from over fifty percent to thirteen percent. It is now below ten percent.

In the National Literacy Campaign, individual posters were produced for each letter of the alphabet—here h for *hamaca* **(hammock).**

Father Fernando Cardenal—the Catholic priest who directed the National Literacy Campaign of 1979.

The campaign was not seen as an end in itself. It was just a beginning, with literacy being the first step towards educating the people. From 1980 on, classes were held to improve the reading of those who had learned the basics. For those who could read, classes at elementary and secondary level were started. Education was made a priority in Nicaragua—not just for the young for whom new schools and colleges were built— but for all. Friendly countries were prepared to accept Nicaraguan students for further, or special, studies. In Cuba, secondary schools were set aside on the Isle of Youth, solely for Nicaraguan students.

69

There was to be another literacy campaign in Nicaragua. The first campaign dealt with the Spanish-speakers, the majority in the country. The English-speakers and Miskito Indians living along the Atlantic coast began their own campaign at the end of 1980, so that they, too, could take their first steps in education.

7

Living in Nicaragua

Before 1979, living conditions throughout Nicaragua were poor. However, the standard of living was higher in the towns and cities (where medical services and education were concentrated) than in the country areas where there was little in the way of health care or schooling. There, infectious diseases, parasites, and illnesses which came from malnutrition were all too common. The mortality rate among babies was high; life expectancy was low.

Curanderos (curers) were frequently resorted to in the countryside. These were people who had a reputation for curing illnesses or diseases, and *campesinos* preferred to consult a *curandero* than travel to a health center which was usually expensive and a considerable distance away. Many Nicaraguans associated disease with natural things like food, the weather, heat or cold, or with snake bites—a common ailment. In the more remote, cut-off areas, even today, people may blame a local witch or sorcerer for the cause of an illness.

Living conditions are still desperately poor in some parts of Nicaragua. This woman and her family have no luxuries.

Curanderos operated openly, using medicines bought from a pharmacy, or herbs, or their own secret remedies. Some specialized in snake bites and many people, if bitten, would seek a *curandero* rather than a doctor. Other traditional forms of treatment were practiced by *sobadoras* who specialized in massage for pregnant women, and the setting of broken bones. The Indians had their own remedies. The *santiguar* of the Matagalpar Indians would make the sign of the cross and recite prayers as part of the treatment of his patients.

In the countryside, superstitions and folk-lore were also important where health was concerned. A pregnant woman, for example, would be afraid to look at a person who had been bitten by a snake, thinking that to do so could result in death. In most villages and towns, an untrained midwife, very often using unsanitary, unhygienic methods, would attend each birth. Perhaps this was one of the reasons for the high death rate among small babies.

These traditional methods of health care had to be brought up to date by the Sandinista government which made health a priority. Health centers were set up in all the towns and cities, with clinics in the countryside. Mobile centers and even boats were sent to the more remote parts of the country. Whereas before 1979 only those who could afford to pay received any medical attention, now the service was for all and provided free.

Nurses were trained and health *brigadistas*, like the *brigadistas* in the Literacy Campaign, traveled to the country districts to begin the task of ensuring decent water supplies, better health

A patient receiving medical aid. Moves to improve the nation's health mean that people in remote country districts now receive treatment from health visitors.

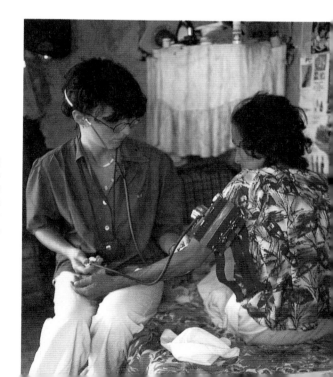

education, the recognition of diseases, the identification of parasites and their elimination, and the wiping out of malaria. The local midwives were also given medical training.

The CDS's–Sandinista Defence Committees–were active in every neighborhood, building the new clinics. They even built new public lavatories to improve hygiene. Vaccination campaigns against measles and polio, and campaigns against the malarial mosquitoes were all begun by the CDS's. All factories and farms began to receive information about, and help in, establishing safer and more hygienic work places.

The miserable standard of living and poor diet were the causes of much ill health before 1979. To improve either would begin the attack on disease and raise health standards. New crops were introduced to add to the diet and improve health. New jobs were created, giving poor people incomes which enabled them to live better. Women were encouraged to breast feed their babies rather than feed them with powdered milk that frequently had to be mixed with contaminated water.

Housing was a much more long-term problem for the government to solve. Managua still had to be rebuilt after the earthquakes of 1972 and it was calculated that a quarter of a million new homes would be needed to deal with the problem of overcrowding.

The new government sought to redress the old imbalance and inequality between the towns and the country and to make life easier for country people in a number of ways. In the country, few houses had running water or sewage systems, and none had

With the old Nicaraguan Cathedral in the background, a young boy sits atop a tree at sunrise. He spends every day watching over his father's two mules and has never attended school.

electricity. In addition, there were no health or education facilities; the people suffered a miserably poor diet and harsh and unremitting toil on the land. Life for those in the towns was always better: wages were higher, and there were transport facilities and even schools.

For most of the population, the major problem was malnutrition. They did not have enough to eat, nor did they always eat the right things. The Sandinista government was to launch a program to improve food production and distribution. Much of the country's food was imported from abroad; the new government looked at ways of making Nicaragua self-sufficient. Foodstuffs went rotten due to the lack of adequate storage facilities or refrigeration; the government centers worked to

75

One of the markets in Managua.

minimize the waste which was especially serious during the rainy season.

Even in the country, the people did not understand what made a good diet. Little fruit was eaten except mangoes and oranges. Vegetables, although often grown on small plots, were not taken seriously as part of the diet. And even where foods were available in abundance, they were often spoiled and contaminated through bad handling. Markets, although colorful and lively, were also places where food was likely to deteriorate or suffer from bad handling.

The new government set itself to solve all these problems. But it would take much to restore the health of many people who had lived unhealthy lives. For the young people, however, the government could immediately ensure better food, better clothes, better education and generally better care. If the Sandinista revolution was to keep going, it would, after all, be the young people who would keep it going.

8

The Nicaraguan People

Nicaragua, like other Central American countries, has a shared history with the rest of Latin America. The Spanish language is just one example of the legacy from Spain, while the English spoken on the Mosquito Coast comes from British colonization. Also shared is its history of monoculture; the production of coffee, then of cotton for export, has resulted in poverty on the one hand and, sometimes, great riches on the other.

In the twentieth century Nicaragua, along with the rest of Latin America and the Caribbean, has seen a dramatic rise in population. In the past, Nicaraguans had a high birth rate but the population did not grow because it was matched by a high death rate, especially among infants.

Under the Somozas, reforms were introduced which lowered the death rate. The result was an explosion in numbers. By the 1970s the birth rate was so high that, if it continued, Nicaragua's population would double every twenty years. That was not such a problem as it seems because Nicaragua had room for

Nicaraguan children run and dance in the streets during the festival of San Marcos.

expansion. However, the changes introduced by the Sandinistas in the 1980s, promoting better health and education, mean that the high birth rates will probably not continue, as people see less need for large families.

With the increase in its population, Nicaragua saw the growth of towns and cities—an experience shared by other poor countries of the world throughout the twentieth century. Without the shift from the country to the towns and cities, the Sandinista revolution would probably not have taken place, for it was the revolt in the towns which sealed Somoza's fate in 1978 and 1979. But the growth of towns and cities poses the problem of providing work for all those who want it. After all, the reason people move to the towns is to improve their standard of living. In Nicaragua today, the government tries to attract people back to the countryside by providing better health care and education,

79

A young *mestizo* boy in Managua. His family, like many others, has left the country and come to live in the city.

and more opportunities for jobs. Once the flow started, however, it has proved difficult, if not impossible, to stop people moving from the countryside to the towns.

The people of the Atlantic coast pose another problem. Their lives are culturally and racially different from the rest of Nicaragua. Even before the arrival of the Spaniards, the inhabitants of the Atlantic coast were of a different race from those of western Nicaragua. Then, when the British established a foothold on Nicaragua, Black slaves were introduced. Today most of the people on the Atlantic coast speak English, or Indian languages, rather than the Spanish spoken by the rest of the population. Their religion is different: Protestant rather than

Roman Catholic. And their culture is different from the rest of the country.

It is because of their history that the Atlantic coast people did not rally to the Sandinistas' cause. From the British time onwards, the coastal people, *costeños*, came to mistrust the "Spaniards" as they described the people of western Nicaragua. Their feeling of being different was made worse by the Somozas who used them in large numbers in the National Guard because of their dislike of Nicaraguans from the west. Few *costeños* followed Sandino in the 1930s or joined the Sandinistas in the 1970s.

A woman police officer. Women have an active role in all areas of life in Nicaragua today.

"Nicaragua is two countries—the Pacific and the Atlantic" is a saying often heard in Nicaragua and the division still remains despite the Sandinistas' attempts to bring the Atlantic people into the revolution. In the north of the Atlantic coast region the Miskito Indians are the largest group, while on the coast itself are found English-speaking Black people, descendants of slaves brought by the British. Small groups of Sumo and Rama Indians live near the Honduran border and in the south. Their mistrust of the west continued towards the Sandinistas. "Somoza neglected us, but at least he left us alone" reflected the feelings of many toward the revolution. The feelings of mistrust were used by those who wished to put a stop to the revolution in Nicaragua, and some Miskito Indians were recruited into the ranks of the *Contras*. The problem of the Atlantic coast was one of the ones the Sandinistas failed to solve.

Other divisions between Nicaraguan people that existed under Somoza have been tackled by subsequent governments. *Machismo,* which puts men first in everything and women in the background, could not be accepted in a new society that had been won by all the people. Women had fought against Somoza and had led troops into battle. It was clear, now that the revolution was under way, that they would not be prepared to take a back seat. Women made up more than 60 percent of those involved in the Literacy Campaign and had active roles in all areas of life; in the army, the police and the People's Militias. Some still hold important positions in the government.

Divisions between the "haves" and the "have nots" also had to be tackled. Most Nicaraguans, wherever they lived, lived in poverty and ignorance. The privileged minority were able to travel abroad and import expensive luxuries. Their only contact with the rest of Nicaragua was through work; they would employ them as workers or servants. Once the revolution was a reality, many rich Nicaraguans simply sold up and left the country. The Sandinistas tried to reassure the former privileged of Nicaragua that their support was necessary if all the people were to enjoy a future together.

9

Religion and Culture

Nicaragua has much in common with other Latin American countries—like its language, Spanish, and its religion, Roman Catholicism. But there are many other cultural characteristics that reflect Nicaragua's unique and very special history. Indian words in the everyday language continue to show the Indian legacy. Indian tribes inhabited Nicaragua and developed a thriving society and culture long before the arrival of the Spaniards. The Coastal English spoken on the Atlantic coast reflects the intrusion of British colonists while some words in the language come from the U.S. occupation and involvement in the affairs of Nicaragua.

As durable as the Spanish language is that other import from Spain—Roman Catholicism. Under the Sandinista revolution, religion became more important and took on a new face. Catholic priests, like Ernesto Cardenal, Fernando Cardenal and Miguel d'Escoto, held important government

Despite his reservations about the major role taken by some Roman Catholic priests in the Nicaraguan revolution, the Pope held an open-air mass in Managua in 1983. (Note the Sandinista propaganda in the background).

positions, putting the Church, despite disapproval by the Pope, in the forefront of change in Nicaragua. Catholic priests were loud in their condemnation of the Somozas in the 1970s, in the period of growing opposition to the Somozas and the National Guard.

Saints' Days are enthusiastically celebrated, with each city, town and village holding its own festivities. Unique in Latin America is the annual week-long festival of *La Purisma* (more important in Nicaragua than Christmas itself), which comes to an end on December 8th. At the time of *La Purisma* altars to the Virgin Mary are erected in each home. Children especially enjoy the festivities as they go from altar to altar saying prayers and singing hymns—for which they are rewarded with good things to eat. Sugarcane is an important gift to the children at this time. Even during the war against Somoza, *La Purisma* was celebrated by the people.

Traditional music dates from pre-Columbian times as well as from the time of the Spanish Conquest. The religious festival of El Atabal in Granada (in honor of Our Lady of the Rosary) has, as its central part, heralds traveling around the city singing verses that were taken to Nicaragua from Spain. In areas of the coast, stringed instruments, like guitars, mandolins and violins

Stringed instruments like those shown here are traditionally used in performing Nicaraguan music.

are part of a traditional industry as well as providing a popular form of music. In the town of El Sauce, bandoleons, like mandolins, with a leather sound chamber, are the traditional instrument both made and played.

As in the rest of Central America, the Indian people of Nicaragua have made a strong and lasting contribution to the culture of their country through their music, dance and crafts. The Dance to the Sun, and Hymns to the Sons of the Moon are traditionally performed at times of birth, death, weddings and harvest, especially in the provinces of Segovia, Chontales and Matagalpa. Granada is also famous for its Indian dances. The *Baile de los Diabolitos* (Dance of the Devils) is performed in October. An old couple lead the "devils" who are decked out in brilliant costumes, wearing devil masks and Indian headdresses. This dance, snaking through the streets, comes from the earliest years of Spanish rule in Nicaragua. In Masaya, *Las Inditas* (the Little Indian Women) perform a dance of love and courtship. *El Toro Guaco* (the Bull) tells, in dance, the eighteenth-century story of the capture and presentation of a bull to San Jeronimo (Saint Jerome) by a rich farmer, in return for curing him of an illness. *Zopilote* (the Buzzard) is a dance involving Nicaragua's birds of prey. All these dances maintain the rich cultural tradition of Nicaragua, especially that of its Indian peoples. In the towns and cities, dances are more modern. Here the waltz, the tango and bolero are popular, along with the *cumbia,* the *merengue,* and the latest dances from around the world.

Nicaraguan food has much in common with the rest of Central America and Mexico. Maize is a main food ingredient for most of the *campesinos*, and is also used to make a variety of drinks. *Rosquillas*, made with maize and cheese, is a popular staple dish. *Tortillas* (maize pancakes) are eaten everywhere and used as a container for different meats or bean dishes. Beans are an important ingredient in the diet and make up for the lack of protein as found in meat and fish. *Gallo Pinto*, spotted rooster with red beans fried with rice, is a favorite dish, as is *nacatamal*, made of maize dough, rice, tomatoes, chili, potatoes and meat all wrapped in a large leaf. The large leaves, like those from a banana tree, are also used in *veho*, where meat and vegetables in layers, wrapped in the leaves, is slowly steamed in a large pot.

This girl is cooking *tortillas* (maize pancakes which are eaten throughout Nicaragua).

Many people add fiery *salsa de chile* (chili sauce) and *salsa de cebolla* (onion sauce) to every dish.

Food and drink are important throughout the year in Nicaragua. Not surprisingly, since Nicaragua is an important coffee-grower, coffee is the national beverage, drunk with milk at breakfast time but at all other times black and very sweet in small cups. A Nicaraguan can drink apparently limitless amounts of coffee. *Chicha* is a more powerful and stimulating alcoholic drink made from maize. The country also produces a very sweet, strong rum called *Flor de Caña* (flower of the cane). Usually with drinks like *chicha,* rum and beer, *bocas* (literally mouthfuls or snacks) are offered. These could be seafood like big shrimp, *seviche* (raw fish in lemon juice), turtles' eggs, or pieces of meat. Bars try to excel one another in the *bocas* they offer.

Nicaraguans take great pride in the writers and artists that their country has produced. During the Sandinista revolution, the Nicaraguan Ministry of Culture was active in stimulating interest in the arts, music, dance and literature, so as to make people more aware of their country's history and achievements. Cultural *brigadas* (brigades) went out from the towns to the country regions to perform and to collect and record the songs and dances of the different regions. The culture of the Miskito, Suma and Rama Indians has been brought to the rest of the country in television programs. Just as the Sandinista revolution put control of their own affairs back into Nicaraguan hands, so too it encouraged the development of a greater interest in all forms of Nicaraguan culture.

Nicaragua's most famous poet, Ruben Dario (1867-1916) created an original form of poetry called *modernismo* (modernism) which influenced the whole of Latin American literature. Today, Nicaragua is still famous for its poetry. Ernesto Cardenal, the priest and former government minister, is as well-known for his poetry as he is for his religious community at Solentiname.

Shots last night

Some shots were heard last night.
Down by the cemetery.
No one knows whom they killed—or how many.
No one knows anything.

Ernesto Cardenal—
Catholic priest, former
government minister
and poet.

Some shots were heard last night.
And that is all.

Ernesto Cardenal
Epigram XIX

Even Nicaragua's former president has published poetry:

The Fruit

When the sowers decided
to cultivate the fields
they knew that they would have to clear
the stones
the thorns
the weeds.
That they would bloody their hands
and cut their feet.
That they would have to be careful
of the gnawing locusts
and the rats.
That the clean up would be hard
but that finally
against all odds
they would reap a harvest...

Daniel Ortega

10

Nicaragua in the World

Before the 1979 Sandinista revolution, Nicaragua's future was tied closely to that of the United States. The Somoza family had thrown in their lot with America and the two countries had especially close relations. The United States saw the Somozas as their friends; the Somozas looked to the United States for help and support. Only at the end of the 1970s was that help and support not forthcoming; without it, Somoza could not stay in power.

The Sandinistas took over Nicaragua with the intention of establishing better relations with the United States based on "dignity and respect." The new government tried to heal the wounds that existed due to the United States' earlier support of the Somozas and hoped that new relations between the two countries would become a model for the whole of Central America. Alas, it was not to be. The U.S. government of President Reagan cut back its aid and put obstacles in the way of Nicaragua obtaining loans from the world's banks.

Nicaragua's close relations with the United States in the past led to the adoption of "American" pastimes and sports. These Managuans are playing baseball.

In 1981 President Reagan gave $19 million to finance attacks against the Sandinistas. Attacks on Nicaragua increased dramatically. Factories were bombed, fields set alight. Nicaraguan airports and planes were sabotaged. *Contras* operating from Honduras began to attack towns close to the border; many were killed.

The Sandinistas responded by mobilizing the country against the attacks. The people volunteered to defend their country. But the people who volunteered insisted that they were not a "warmongering people." On the contrary it was peace they desperately wanted. Having to be concerned with defence

These children have lost their homes, and many their parents too, in the war waged by the *Contras*.

meant that the essential task of rebuilding Nicaragua after the war against Somoza was put back. Schools were forced to close, teachers killed, health centers destroyed. Attempts to develop new industries, to build new schools, and to build a new Nicaragua were all frustrated. This has cost Nicaragua dear, as has the damage caused directly by the Contras. In 1982 this amounted to more than $60 million; by the end of 1983 to more than $2 billion.

Other Latin American countries came to the assistance of Nicaragua. The Contadora group of countries—Mexico, Colombia, Panama and Venezuela—first met on the Panamanian island of Contadora in January 1983. Their aim was to find a solution to the problems of Central America, which have caused 150,000 people to lose their lives in the seven years to 1985, in wars or from Death Squads. This group saw peace coming to Central America, particularly Nicaragua, El Salvador and Guatemala, only when force was replaced by peaceful coexistence, mutual respect, and above all, an end to intervention from outside. While many governments around the world agreed that the Contadora proposals held out the best chance for peace in the area, the United States government, in 1985, was not prepared to support them.

After the elections in 1984, the new president, Daniel Ortega, offered the Contras an amnesty. However, this was rejected.

Part of the reason for the United States' suspicions of the Sandinistas was that they established new trade and diplomatic contacts around the world, some of them with countries like the former Soviet Union, Cuba and Vietnam. The Nicaraguans were trying to lessen their dependence and reliance on trade with the United States: in this regard they were to face their greatest challenge, given the $1.6 billion debt inherited from Somoza. But considerable progress has been made in developing new trading partners and obtaining loans to be used in building the new Nicaragua. Only by establishing new crops and new products, which can then be sold to a multitude of markets, can Nicaragua be truly independent and set its own course.

Free elections were held in Nicaragua on November 4, 1984. Although there was a large voter turnout and the Sandinistas won a majority of the votes, some opposition groups refused to participate. United States opposition to the Nicaraguan regime grew.

The eventual resolution of the conflicts in Central America came about through local efforts. In 1986 Oscar Arias Sanchez was elected president of Costa Rica. He was determined to end the ongoing civil wars in Nicaragua, El Salvador, and Guatemala. The Arias peace plan called for a ceasefire, amnesty, and end to foreign aid for the warring factions, and a regional economic development program. Although Arias was awarded the Nobel Peace Prize in 1987, the various conflicts dragged on for a few more years.

As the 1990 election approached, Nicaragua faced a new situation. The other Central American civil wars were winding down, United States aid for the Contras had been discontinued, and the Nicaraguan people were weary of war and hardship.

A large political coalition formed in Nicaragua that was both anti-Sandinista and anti-Contra. The 14-party coalition, known as the Union Nacional Opositora (UNO), was led by Violetta de Barrios Chamorro. While they had expected to do well, the world was stunned when the UNO won the election on February 25, 1990.

Although international aid was increased, Nicaragua's recovery from revolution and civil war has been slow. Maintaining strong support in some sections of the population, the Sandinistas have cooperated with the UNO government in many areas of Nicaraguan life. New elections in 1996 brought the presidency to

Daniel Ortega, former president of Nicaragua.

Arnoldo Aleman, who pursued policies similar to those of Violetta Chamorro. The new government is trying to expand tourism, encourage private investment, and make progress toward reducing the large national debt.

GLOSSARY

campesinos	Country people who own small farms.
chacras	Small family plots of land not owned by the wealthy landowners.
chicha	An alcoholic drink made from maize (corn).
Contras	Anti-Sandinista guerrillas, supported by the United States, who waged a war against the Nicaraguan government during the 1980s.
costenos	Residents of Nicaragua's eastern coast, who are primarily Black or Indian.
curanderos	Native healers found in rural areas who often use herbs or magic for cures.
haciendas	Large estates.
huertas	Small, sufficient farms.
junta	Literally a "meeting," in Latin America usually a governing committee, often dictatorial or ruling in an emergency situation.
maize	Indian corn.
mestizo	A person of mixed Spanish and Indian descent.
Mosquitia	Also known as the Moskito or Mosquito Coast,

this eastern region of Nicaragua has been heavily influenced by its former British rulers.

quapote A primitive fish found in Nicaraguan lakes.

quetzal A brightly plumed bird of Central America, sacred in some Indian cultures.

Sandinistas A revolutionary movement formed in 1961, drawing inspiration from the career of Augusto Cesar Sandino(1893-1934). The Sandinistas ruled Nicaragua from 1979 to 1990.

sharks A large predatory fish; Nicaragua's lakes have the world's only freshwater sharks.

tortillas Pancakes made from maize (corn).

INDEX

pirates, 26, 31
poetry, 23, 90-91
population, 7, 13, 15, 28-29, 53, 78
Presidential Palace, 16, 41
Prinzapolka River, 17
Puerto Sandino (formerly Puerto
    Somoza), 18

Q
quapote, 22, 26
quetzal, 24

R
railways, 17
rainfall, 17
Rama Indians, 82, 89
Reagan, President Ronald, 61, 92-93
rebuilding work, 53, 94
religion, 7, 45, 47, 80, 84-91
Rio Grande, 17
Rio Viejo valley, 24
rivers, 7, 13, 17, 26
roads, 17, 37, 53
Roman Catholic Church, 45, 54, 57,
    68, 81, 84, 85

S
Sacaso, Edgard Lang, 45
Sacasa, President, 40
San Carlos, 26
Sanchez, Oscar Arias, 96
Sandinista Defence Committees
    (CDS's), 55, 74
Sandinista National Liberation Front
    (FSLN), 10, 11, 43, 45, 48, 49, 50,
    53, 54, 55
Sandinista organizations, 11, 55, 79

Sandinista, revolution of, 11, 19, 39,
    40, 42, 45-52, 63, 79, 81, 82, 92
Sandinista flag, 55
Sandino, Augusto Cesar, 10, 38, 39-
    41, 81
San Juan del Notre, 26
San Juan River, 7, 9, 14, 26
schools, 9
slavery, slaves, 29, 30, 32, 34, 35,
    58, 80, 82
social reforms, 43, 54
Somoza Debayle, Luis, 10, 11, 42,
    43
Somoza family, 10, 11, 20, 39, 41-
    52, 62, 78-79, 82, 85
Somoza Garcia, Anastasio (1936-56),
    10, 41
Somoza Debayle, Anastasio (1967-
    79), 11, 43-52
Somoza regime, 10, 11, 20, 39, 41-
    52, 62, 78, 79, 82, 85
Spain, Spaniards, 10, 23, 25, 28, 29,
    30, 31, 32, 34, 59, 70
Spanish Conquest, 28-34, 58, 86
Spanish language, 7, 70, 78, 84
standard of living, 42, 43, 61, 63, 71,
    74, 79
sugarcane, 8, 23, 26, 54, 86
Sumo Indians, 82, 89
strikes, 45, 48

T
timber, 32, 37
Tipitapa River, 14, 22
tobacco, 25, 58
tortillas, 88
trade unions, 55

transportation, 17, 26, 54
Treaty of Paris, 9

U

unemployment, 53, 60
Union Nacional Opositora (UNO), 11, 96
United States Marines, 39
United States occupations, 10, 39, 84
United States, 9, 11, 19, 34, 35, 36, 37, 38, 39, 40, 42, 47, 56, 62, 64, 92, 95

V

vegetation, 24

Vietnam, 57, 95
volcanoes, 7, 9, 13, 14, 20, 21, 22, 25, 26
von Humboldt, Alexander, 34

W

Walker, William, 26, 35, 36
Wallace, Peter, 31
war, 10, 17, 40
wildlife, 24, 26
women, status of, 55, 57, 82

Z

Zelaya, José Santos, 37-38
Zeledon, Benjamin, 38